MAGICAL
stories for
GIRLS

MAGICAL
stories for
GIRLS

WRITTEN BY
Nicola Baxter

ILLUSTRATED BY
Cathie Shuttleworth & Belinda Lyon

ARMADILLO

This edition published in 2005 by Armadillo Books
An imprint of Bookmart Limited
Registered Number 2372865
Trading as Bookmart Ltd
Blaby Road, Wigston
Leicestershire, LE18 4SE
England

ISBN 1 84322 456 9

This material was taken from the following titles
previously published by Bookmart Ltd
My Book of Princess Stories
Fairy Tales from the Brothers Grimm
My Magical Pony Tales Collection

Printed in Dubai

CONTENTS

The Magical Tale of

THE PONY OF THE NORTH WIND

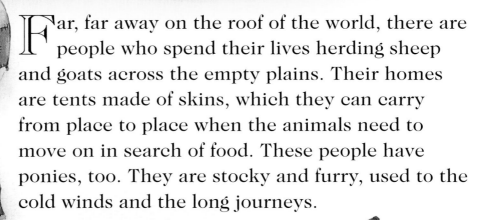

Far, far away on the roof of the world, there are people who spend their lives herding sheep and goats across the empty plains. Their homes are tents made of skins, which they can carry from place to place when the animals need to move on in search of food. These people have ponies, too. They are stocky and furry, used to the cold winds and the long journeys.

But it is not of these ponies that the grandmothers tell the little ones, when they are all huddled around the fire at night. They speak of the pony of the north wind—a white pony with a flowing mane and tail, whose hoofs are of silver and so light they hardly make a sound upon the cold earth. This is the pony of the north wind. This is the pony that brings the snow.

"You must listen, my children," say the grandmothers, "and look out at the sky. When the clouds are heavy and dull and the wind begins to moan, listen hard for the sound of silver hoofs. It is like no other sound you will ever hear. It is in the silence when the wind is still for a moment. It is in the breathing of the beasts as they shift and stray. It is in the beating of your hearts. When you hear those silver hoofs, you must pitch your tents and stay close to your mothers. For the north wind is galloping and bringing the snow."

The children smiled at what the grandmothers said. Spring was coming. It seemed a long, long time before the pony of the north wind would gallop by their tents again.

"I don't believe there is such a pony," said a little boy called Ula. "Ponies don't have silver hoofs. They can't move along without making a sound. I don't believe it at all."

The grandmothers shivered and shook their heads. They didn't like to hear someone speak so of something he did not understand.

Spring came at last. It was still cold on the wide, open plains, and the winds blew as strongly as ever, but the stocky little ponies that grazed around the camps became sleeker. The sparse,

tough grass grew a little longer. The sheep and goats looked healthy and plump. Soon little lambs and kids were standing with their mothers, testing their wobbly legs on the hard, flat ground. The children helped the herders to keep the little ones safe from wild dogs and lions.

Summer swept over the plains leaving scarcely a trace. Only a few shy flowers nodded their tiny heads in the sunlight. The wild wind never stopped. It ruffled the manes of the ponies and battered at the tents, begging to be let in. Inside, safe and warm in the light evenings, the old women began to talk of the autumn and the cold. It was coming, they said. They could feel it in their bones.

"It is time we were moving south again," they said. "For the cold winds are coming closer every day."

Once again the herds moved on and the herders with them. The children's red cheeks glowed in the freshening wind. Their black hair streamed out behind them as they ran beside the animals. The little brown ponies lowered their heads and hunched their shoulders against the cold. The nights grew darker.

It was a little girl who first noticed that the boy Ula had gone. With watering eyes, she stared across the plains, but there was no sign of him. The grandmothers hung their heads and sighed. No one could survive by himself in the weather that was coming.

"We warned him," they said. "For him, knowledge will come too late."

Far away, alone on the wind-whipped plain, Ula heard his own heart beating. It frightened him. He listened to the moaning of the wind and thought he heard … something … a pulse, a beat, a drumming on the earth. He knelt and put his ear to the hard ground, hoping to pick up the sound of his own people and find the direction they had gone. But all he could hear was his own breath, hot against his hand, and the thudding of his own heart, fast and fearful.

As night began to fall, the full moon slid up into the sky. In the cavern of deepest blue, a million sparkling stars shimmered coldly. Ula hugged a blanket around his shoulders. He had not eaten for hours. His legs felt heavy and dead. He had never felt so alone.

Then, in the silence of the stars and the silver light of the moon, he heard something. It was a whisper at first. It was like a tingling in his frozen fingers. It was like a singing in his dreaming head. It pounded like his heart, like his breathing, like the blood through his veins. Almost too cold to move, he turned, knowing what he would see.

The pony of the north wind was fearsome. It moved like the lashing of a winter storm. Its hoofs made no sound on the earth, but little bright sparks flew up where they struck. Its mane streamed out behind it, cold as ice and furious as flame. But its eyes … its eyes were glinting with cold. Ula looked into them and felt his blood freeze. He closed his pale eyes and dropped to the ground like a falling star. He was still.

Behind the pony came the snow. Soft, white flakes covered the boy, wrapping him safe in a blanket of snow. And the pony of the north wind swept on over the plain, catching the herders in their tents, chilling the grandmothers as they huddled by the fire, making their dark eyes fill with tears as they grieved for the boy who was lost.

But Ula didn't feel the cold. The icy wind passed through him and he smiled. His spirit soars in the wind now. He lives in the moaning of the wind and the sighing of the stars. And he rides the pony of the north wind, never sorry, never still.

The Princess and the Unicorn

Once upon a time, there was a very beautiful Princess. She lived in a fairytale castle, surrounded by the prettiest gardens you have ever seen. She had everything that a Princess could desire, and she was a very clever girl too. But—and this is very strange—she didn't believe in magic!

Now in stories, Princesses are always coming across good fairies and bad fairies, witches and wizards, elves and pixies. They meet frogs who can talk and little men who can spin straw into gold. In fact, there seems to be magic all over the place.

But this Princess, whose name was Cariana, had never seen a fairy or an elf. No one had put a spell on her to send her to sleep for a hundred years. She had not been imprisoned by a witch. Her cat and her dog meowed and barked but did not say a word in human language. So perhaps it was not really surprising that she did not believe in magic at all.

"I'll believe in it," she said with a laugh, "when I can see it with my own eyes, and not until then."

One day, Princess Cariana went for a walk in the woods. It was a beautiful, sunny day. The birds sang in the trees and her little dog, Plum, enjoyed sniffing here and there among the roots of the trees and burying his nose in the woodland flowers.

"Who needs magic when the real world is so beautiful?" The Princess smiled.

Perhaps it was because she was feeling so happy that the young Princess walked further than she ever had before. It seemed that the further she went, the more lovely the trees and flowers became. Surely the sunlight had never sparkled so brightly? Every leaf and flower seemed to have its own golden light, and a sweet perfume filled the air. The Princess could not bear to turn back from such beauty, so she walked on and on. At last she sank down on a flowery bank.

"I will just rest here for a moment," she told her little dog.

Plum snuffled happily under some bushes for a while. When he looked up at the Princess again, she was sleeping peacefully among the flowers. Plum settled down at her feet, but he did not go to sleep. He knew it was his duty to guard his mistress.

The Princess must have been very tired indeed, for she slept for a long time. When she finally opened her eyes, the sun was just setting, and a soft, warm darkness was falling over the woods.

"I must hurry home!" cried the Princess.

Scrambling to her feet, the Princess set off along the path, but it was hard now to see where she was going, although little glowing insects hovered among the trees. After she had taken only a few steps, the Princess caught her foot in a tree root and tumbled to the ground.

"Oh, Plum," she cried, "I have hurt my ankle. I don't think I can walk any further. What will happen to us?" With a sigh, she fainted clean away. (You must remember that she had led a very sheltered life and was not used to having to face difficulties and dangers.)

Plum stood guard over his mistress, looking nervously about him. Suddenly, the woods that had seemed so lovely before became full of strange rustling, breathing noises. There were little squeaks and scufflings that he had never noticed in the daylight. Plum knew that woods might be full of dangerous animals. There could be snakes or wolves or even—and this was a really horrible thought—bears! Sure enough, a second or two later the little dog heard the sound of a really big animal crashing toward him—fast!

As the brave little dog prepared to defend his mistress with his life, a shimmering white shape appeared through the trees. It was a unicorn!

Gently the beautiful white animal lowered his
silver horn and lifted the Princess onto his back.
Then he lowered his head again and looked at
the little dog. Plum thought he had never seen
such kind, wise eyes. He knew at once that
everything would be fine and let himself be
lifted up beside his mistress.

Plum never forgot the magical ride through the
trees that followed. It was as if the unicorn's
hooves hardly touched the ground.

Before long, the lighted castle appeared before them. The unicorn laid the Princess gently in the gardens and vanished into the night.

Now it was Plum's turn. Barking as loudly as he could, he summoned help from the castle.

The Princess's ankle was soon better. Ever afterward, she was careful not to stray too far into the forest, but she had no memory of what had happened.

To this day, the Princess still doesn't believe in magic…

But Plum does!

The Enchanted Tale of
THE FOREST PONIES OF ELFLAND

Elves, as you know, are tiny. They can drink from acorn cups and fill their quilts with thistledown. Their ponies are tiny too, by human standards, but they are much, much bigger than elves. No elf would dream of trying to ride an Elfland pony. Those little people are much more at home perched on the back of a large frog, or a duck, or a rabbit. They twist grasses together to make little bridles and sew leaves together to make saddles. Then up they hop and off they go, with a hop, a waddle, or a jump.

Meanwhile, deep in the forests, the Elfland ponies are hardly ever seen, even by elves. They are completely wild and very shy. Some are a leafy shade of green. Others are dappled brown and yellow and green, like the patterns that sunlight makes when it splashes through the trees.

You could easily walk through an Elfland forest and never see a pony, although dozens of them might be standing quietly by the path, blending with the leaves and branches.

Almost everything in Elfland is magic. The ponies are no exception, but they only use their magic when their country and the elves that live there are threatened. That is what happened when the Wizard of Marr turned his hideous attention towards Elfland.

The Wizard of Marr was evil through and through. Everything his twisted fingers touched died or became ugly. When the goblins rose up and threw him out of his castle on Brooding Peak, he decided to travel across the mountains into Elfland. He hated elves. They were, in his opinion, weak creatures, too nice for their own good.

The elves first knew about the arrival of the Wizard of Marr when a horrible dusty wind blew into their homes and covered everything in a layer of thick, evil-smelling ash. The wizard had set fire to the wonderful rolling wheatfields that stretched from the foot of the mountains to the edge of the forests. Before long, the elves could smell the burning from their tree-trunk homes.

"If the flames reach the forest, we are finished," said Elderberry. "What can we possibly do?"

"We can beat out the flames with sticks and carry water from our wells," said Holly bravely. But she knew that it was hopeless.

Nevertheless, the next morning, a band of twenty little elves set out. The Wizard of Marr, viewing them through his magic telescope, laughed softly. With a wave of his hand, he put out the flames, leaving an ugly burnt path to show where he had been.

Above the little party of elves, the smoky air cleared. Elderberry scrambled to the top of a tree and looked out over the fields.

"The fire has stopped," he said, "but a huge black cloud is moving this way. Let's go back to our homes. Quickly!"

No sooner had the elves shut themselves into the hollowed-out houses than a frightening storm exploded overhead. Thunder rattled the windows. Lightning crackled alarmingly. And rain lashed at the forest like arrows from a furious army. The elves huddled in their homes, watching as leaves and branches blew past outside.

"Such a storm has never been known in Elfland," said Holly's father, Hawthorn. "We can't take much more of this. I've been thinking. This storm isn't natural, you know. Some evil force is attacking us, and there is nothing that we can do about it. Look out!"

A huge branch hurtled through the window and missed the little family by inches. Through the broken panes, the rain lashed viciously at everything it could touch. Between the roaring of the thunder and the snapping of the lightning, another sound could be heard. It was low and soft. It made the hair stand up on the back of your neck and cold trickles run down your spine. It was a while before the elves realized what it was. Someone was laughing.

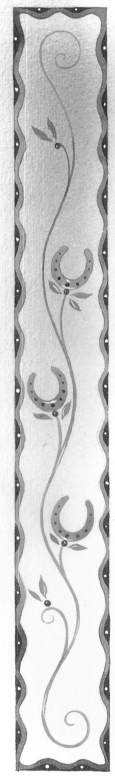

All this time, the ponies had been shifting restlessly in the forest. Their keen nostrils smelled the smoke and they shied nervously. When the storm came, they huddled under the trees, their heads resting on each other's backs.

But as the Wizard of Marr drew closer, the ponies felt his evil. They could sense the sick sweetness of his magic slithering across the mossy ground towards them. They lifted their heads and faced the enemy.

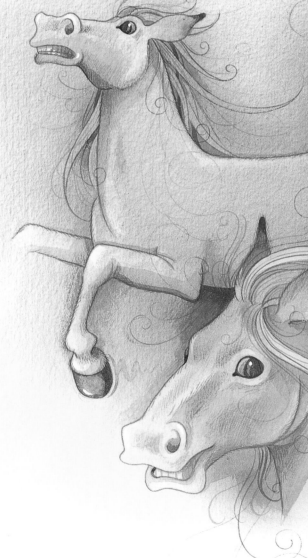

There was no signal. There was no sound. But suddenly the ponies began to move as one, galloping towards the source of the danger like a green, foaming sea. Their thudding hoofs drowned the thunder. Their tossing manes shook off the rain. Faster and faster they galloped, brushing lightly past the elves' homes on the edge of the forest, surging towards the mountains, feeling the wizard's evil closer with every step.

The Wizard of Marr, laughing in the face of the storm and thinking only of the harm that he could do, did not notice the ponies until it was too late. Suddenly, their hoofs were on the hem of his robes. He felt their hot breath on his cheek. But he could not see them. His twisted mind refused to see the tide of goodness that swept towards him. All he felt was a terrible faintness as his power drained from him.

That evening, all was still in the forests of Elfland. In the glow of the setting sun, the elves began to repair the damage that the storm had done. Deep in the forest, the ponies melted into the shadows once more. And at the foot of the mountains, a very old and feeble man in tattered robes began to climb.

A Dress for a Princess

There was once a Princess who really enjoyed being royal. She loved having servants to do everything she said. She adored the rich foods served on golden plates. She liked living in a magnificent palace. And most of all, she liked the beautiful clothes she could wear. There was a whole corridor lined with doors bearing the royal coat of arms. And behind those doors there were more dresses and cloaks and satin slippers than you can imagine.

But in spite of all her lovely clothes, Princess Pomona always wanted more. One day, she heard that her cousin, Princess Pandora, was getting married. She was quite, quite determined to have the most gorgeous dress there. After all, every Princess for miles around would be present, and they would *all* be wearing their very finest clothes.

The Princess lost no time in summoning the Royal Dressmaker. She made it perfectly clear that she wanted something much more beautiful than her very best dresses.

The dressmaker listened carefully. "Do you mean something like this, Your Royal Highness?" she asked, making a quick sketch.

"Oh no!" cried Princess Pomona. "Much finer than that. And definitely a lot more lace and gold thread around here."

So the Royal Dressmaker made another sketch. And Princess Pomona suggested a few more alterations—and then a few more.

It was lucky that the wedding was still some months away because there was a lot to be done. A special Royal Messenger was sent to China for some beautiful golden silk. Another set off for Paris to find the exact shade of rose satin that was needed for the wonderful dress.

Meanwhile, pearls were ordered from India. Opals began the journey from Africa. And in Belgium, four hundred lacemakers started work on yards and yards of gold lace. The Royal Dressmaker had many a sleepless night as she tried to work out how to finish the dress on time.

A huge room of the palace was set aside for the Royal Dressmaker and her team of fifty seamstresses to set to work. They worked from dawn to dusk, but when night fell, even the brightest lamps were not strong enough to allow them to see the tiny stitches and lacy embroidery of the dress.

One day, the King came to look at the work. He frowned a little. "There's more to being a Princess than fine clothes, you know," he told his daughter. "I hope these workers are enjoying their work as much as you will enjoy the dress."

In fact, there was so much sewing to do that the Princess was not able to try on the finished dress until it was time to set off for the wedding. The Royal Dressmaker had followed her instructions exactly, and the dress really was the most beautiful garment. As Princess Pomona stood before the mirror, she was confident that she would be the most beautifully dressed royal personage at the Grand Ball that was to follow the wedding.

It is true that the dress was rather heavy to wear, but that didn't worry the Princess as she sat in the royal coach beside her father and mother. Actually, the King and Queen were rather squashed, as the skirts of the dress took up most of the room in the carriage.

"Let's hope not everyone is wearing a dress like yours," joked the King, "or there will not be enough room in the cathedral!"

"Don't be silly, Daddy," said his daughter rather sharply. "There won't *be* another dress like mine in the whole of the kingdom."

Well, the wedding was magnificent. And although there were lots and lots of beautiful dresses, not one of them came close to Princess Pomona's gown.

The crowds cheered as the happy couple left the cathedral, but to tell you the truth, they cheered even louder when they saw Princess Pomona's dress. They had never seen anything like it.

As dusk fell, and the chandeliers were lit all over the palace, it was time for the Grand Ball. The musicians took their places. The conductor lifted his baton. The most beautiful swirling music filled the ballroom.

At once, three Princes from nearby kingdoms begged Princess Pomona to give them the first dance. Laughing, she accepted the first one and promised the others to dance with them later. Her feet in their satin slippers were tapping already, as she knew that she could dance beautifully. She couldn't wait to float across the floor.

Oh dear! I'm sorry to say that floating was quite out of the question in *that dress*. It was much too heavy to move in, and poor Princess Pomona was forced to sit down for the rest of the evening.

The dress is in a museum now, which is much the best place for it. And Princess Pomona? I did hear that recently she has sometimes been seen dressed like … *a boy*!

SNOW WHITE AND THE SEVEN DWARFS

O ne cold winter's day, a Queen sat sewing by an open window. Suddenly, she pricked her finger, and a drop of red blood fell on the snow below. The Queen looked down and sighed.

"One day," she whispered, "I would like to have a daughter with skin as white as this snow, lips as red as this blood, and hair as black as this window frame."

Before long, the Queen's wish came true. Her baby daughter looked just as she had imagined, so she called her Snow White. But very shortly afterward, the Queen died, leaving the baby to be brought up by her husband, the King.

The King was heartbroken by his wife's death, but
he soon became lonely. Within a year, he had married
again. The new Queen was extremely beautiful, but
her heart was cold as ice.

Now the Queen had a magic
mirror that she looked into
every day. And every day she
asked the mirror a question:

"Mirror, mirror,
On the wall,
Who is the fairest
One of all?"

The mirror would at once reply:

"O Queen, now I can truly say,
You are the fairest one this day."

Hearing this, the Queen would be satisfied.

Meanwhile, little Snow White was growing up.
Every day she grew more and more beautiful.

So it was that the day came when the mirror gave a reply that made the Queen mad with fury.

"O Queen, your time has passed away,
Snow White is the fairest one this day."

Turning to look at her stepdaughter, the Queen saw the truth of the mirror's words. She hurried through the castle and called for a huntsman.

"Take Snow White into the forest," she told him, "and bring me back her heart to show that she is dead."

Reluctantly, the huntsman did as the wicked woman had said, but when the moment came to kill the girl, he could not bring himself to do it.

"Just leave me here," begged Snow White, sobbing. "I promise that I will never come home."

So the huntsman took back an animal's heart and left Snow White in the dark forest, all alone.

Snow White wandered through the trees for hours. Then, just when she thought she could go no farther, she saw a quaint little cottage. No one came to answer her knock, so she tiptoed inside.

What a curious little house it was! On the table were seven little plates and seven little glasses. In the middle was a basket of bread and fruit. Poor Snow White was so hungry that she took a little food. Then, she climbed up the winding stairs to the bedroom. There she lay down on the first little bed she came to and fell fast asleep.

Several hours later, Snow White was awoken by a sharp little voice.

"Just what do you think you are doing in our house?" it asked.

Snow White looked up to see seven dwarfs, in working clothes, standing around. The young girl took her courage in both hands and explained what had happened to her.

"And now," she said, "I have nowhere to go at all."

"Yes, you do!" chorused the dwarfs. "You can stay here with us!" They told her that they worked all day and needed someone to look after them.

"You will be safe here," they said. "But you must promise us never to open the door to a stranger."

So Snow White stayed
with the dwarfs. She cooked
their meals and cared for
their little house, but her life
was very different from the
one she had lived at home.
She longed for someone to
talk to during the long days.

Then, one fine morning,
her wish came true. An old woman, with a basket of
pretty things, knocked on the cottage door.

Snow White longed to look through the laces and
ribbons in the stranger's basket, but she remembered
her friends' warning. Still, she could not resist talking
to the woman through the open window.

Snow White did not realize that her visitor was none other than the wicked Queen in disguise. For months, the Queen had been so happy that she did not consult her mirror at all. When she did, she had a terrible shock.

"O Queen, you cannot have your will,
For Snow White is the fairest still."

Raging through her kingdom, the Queen had hunted high and low for the missing girl, taking on different disguises. She could scarcely hide her delight at finding her at last.

"You are wise **not** to open the door to strangers, my dear," she smiled. "But to show that there are no hard feelings, please take this shiny red apple as a gift from a new friend."

It seemed impolite to refuse, so Snow White stretched out her hand and took the apple. It looked delicious. Waving goodbye to her visitor, she took one tiny bite.

When the dwarfs returned from their work that evening, they found Snow White lying lifeless on the floor, the apple still clutched in her hand.

"This is the work of the Queen, I'm sure," cried one dwarf, sobbing. "She has robbed us of the sweetest girl in the world."

Sadly, the dwarfs took their friend and placed her in a crystal coffin, taking turns to watch over her night and day. She seemed to grow more lovely as she lay there, silent, cold and still.

One morning, a young Prince rode by and saw the coffin and the beautiful girl inside. He fell in love with her at once and vowed, although she could never be his bride, that he would not be parted from her.

"Let me take her back to my palace," he begged, "where she can lie in state as befits a Princess."

The dwarfs discussed the matter and agreed that she deserved no less. Carefully, they helped the Prince to lift the coffin.

But as they did so, the piece of apple that had caught in Snow White's throat was dislodged. She took one breath and then another. Amid the tears of her friends, she sat up and smiled at the Prince.

You may guess the end of the story. Snow White and her Prince lived happily ever after. And the wicked Queen? She was so eaten up with rage and envy that she died soon after, leaving the young couple to enjoy their happiness in peace.

The Spellbinding Tale of
THE PURPLE DREAM PONY

There are, as I'm sure you know, mountain ponies and forest ponies. There are ponies who race across the wide plains or swim the foaming rivers between rolling, green hills.

But there are also ponies who do not live anywhere in the real world. They are dream ponies, who carry sleeping children to the land of dreams and bring them safely home again when morning comes.

Dream ponies are beautiful. They have long, flowing manes and tails. Their coats are in lovely jewel shades of sapphire, emerald, amethyst and topaz. Their hoofs sparkle like diamonds, but their eyes are soft and kind.

Young dream ponies must learn to take very good care of the children they carry.

"Never let them become frightened," say the older ponies, "by galloping too fast. Take them to the sweetest dreams you can find. And make sure you take them home in plenty of time."

The purple dream pony, ready for her first real mission, listened carefully to these words.

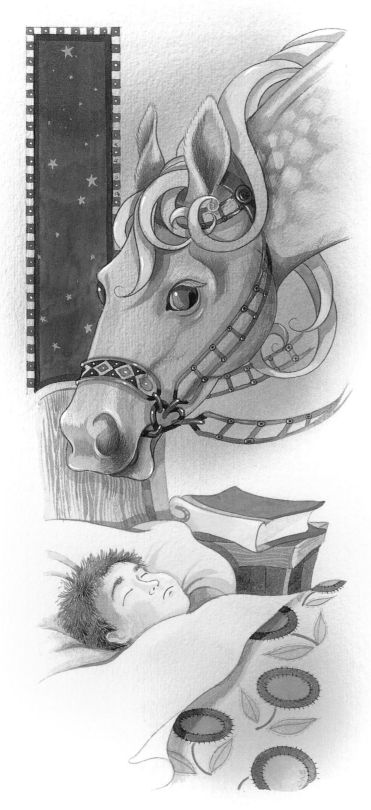

That evening, as the soft dusk fell over the fields, the purple dream pony set off to find the child she would carry to the land of dreams. She waited patiently outside his window, knowing that she must not let him see her while he was still awake.

At last Tom—that was his name—put down his book and closed his eyes. The purple pony entered his room by magic and stood quietly by his bed. Then she gently asked him what kind of dream he would like to have that night.

Tom didn't hesitate. "A dream about castles," he said, "and knights on horseback."

"Climb onto *my* back," smiled the purple pony, "and I'll take you there."

Off they galloped, flying through the night towards a shimmering place among the stars.

"A castle!" cried Tom. "Let me get down and explore! It's just like the one in my book!"

The purple dream pony watched as the little boy ran through the castle, pretending to be a brave knight. She made sure that she could see where he was all the time. It was her job to make sure that this was a good dream.

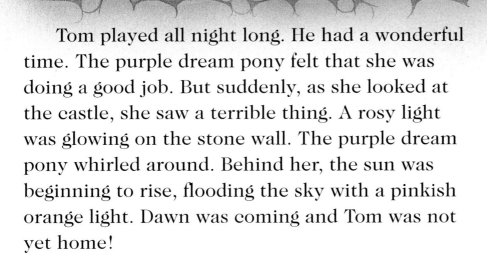

Tom played all night long. He had a wonderful time. The purple dream pony felt that she was doing a good job. But suddenly, as she looked at the castle, she saw a terrible thing. A rosy light was glowing on the stone wall. The purple dream pony whirled around. Behind her, the sun was beginning to rise, flooding the sky with a pinkish orange light. Dawn was coming and Tom was not yet home!

The purple dream pony did not waste a second. She scooped the little boy up onto her back and set off through the glow of early morning.

"But I don't want to go!" wailed Tom. "I was having such a good time!"

The pony felt frightened now. Dreams are wonderful things, but every dream pony must make sure that waking up to a whole new day is just as much fun. No one can live in dreamland all the time.

The purple dream pony flew like the wind. She had to get Tom back to his bed before he awoke and saw her. Birds were singing loudly in Tom's garden as the pony landed gently under his window. The pony was only just in time. As Tom's head hit the pillow, his eyelids began to flutter. He stretched and yawned.

In the daylight, the dream pony faded. You could hardly see her now as she waited anxiously beside Tom's bed. Then the little boy woke up properly and smiled as a delicious smell wafted into the room.

"Pancakes for breakfast!" he cried happily. It was a wonderful dream, but I'm *so* glad to be awake!"

The dream pony sighed with relief—and like the darkness, she faded right away.

Where's That Girl?

The King of Kerling had a problem. He had a clever and beautiful daughter called Princess Pilar. Now this would not be a problem to most Kings, but this particular one found that his daughter tried his patience to the limit. You see, she simply refused to marry any of the Princes he found for her.

"Why should I?" she asked. "I'm perfectly happy as I am. And anyway, those Princes are hopeless! Not one of them can do anything sensible."

"Don't be silly, my dear," said the King. "Princes aren't meant to do anything sensible. They just … well, they just *are*, that's all."

"Well, it's not enough," said Princess Pilar. "After all, what are Princes *for*?"

"They're for marrying Princesses," said the King firmly, "and I insist that you marry the very next one who comes to call."

But the following Saturday, when the *toot-toot-toot* of a herald's trumpet announced the arrival of yet another Prince, Princess Pilar was nowhere to be found.

"Search the castle!" cried the King. "I want that girl found, and I want her found now!"

But although servants scurried to every part of the castle where the Princess might have hidden, they couldn't find so much as a trace of her silken slippers.

"You are all nincompoops!" cried the King, as the breathless servants trooped back into the banqueting hall. "If she isn't *in* the castle, then she's *outside* the castle. Search the grounds!"

So pages ran up and down the gardens, and chamberlains searched the woods, and heralds rowed up and down the river calling (very politely) the name of Princess Pilar. But she was nowhere to be found.

At last the King was forced to apologize to the visiting Prince and send him on his way. And would you believe it, five minutes after the Prince's carriage disappeared over the hill, the Princess strolled into the banqueting hall, looking very calm and collected.

"Where have you been?" cried the King. "I sent servants to look for you everywhere!"

"Not everywhere, obviously," said the Princess coolly, and she strolled off about her business.

The next week, the very same thing happened. The King was furious, but there was nothing he could do. No matter how many people looked for the Princess, they couldn't find her … until the visiting Prince had ridden over the hill, and then she would turn up as if nothing had happened.

So where was the Princess week after week whenever the heralds announced the visit of a Prince? She was in the one place nobody thought of looking, because it was dark and uncomfortable and not in the least bit the kind of place that was suitable for silken shoes or golden coronets. It was the scullery, where the Royal Dishwasher spent all day washing up the golden plates and silver platters from which the King and the Princess dined three times a day.

Of course, the Princess had spent a lot of time in the scullery. And she had spent a lot of time with the Royal Dishwasher, who was a handsome young man.

The King did not know this, so he told the Princess that he needed a serious talk with her. "My dear," he said, "I have your best interests at heart."

"Very well," said the Princess. "I am ready to get married, but you must let me choose the man myself."

"I agree," said the King, confident that his daughter, who was so clever and beautiful, would choose wisely.

And that is how it happened that the Princess of Kerling married the Royal Dishwasher and lived happily ever after.

And although the widowed King took some time to get over the shock, he did eventually feel that his daughter had been right—especially after he himself took a new wife and married the Royal Cook…

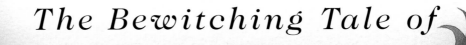

The Bewitching Tale of

THE PRINCESS PONY

When King Hippus struck the ground with his royal hoof, everyone knew he was very cross indeed. When he tossed his mane and let his crown slip over one eye, the other magical ponies shuffled nervously. What was annoying their noble king?

Queen Equestra tried to soothe him.

"My dear," she whinnied gently, "it can't be as bad as that."

"It can and it is!" snorted His Majesty, stamping again. "What did I do to deserve such a tiresome child? She has been nothing but trouble since she stopped being a foal and started being a…"

"A real princess!" his wife interposed quickly. She knew only too well that her husband's royal vocabulary included some quite *impolite* words. "But whatever has she done to upset you now? I've not heard a word from her all day."

"That," snuffled the King, "is the problem."

He looked out of the window of the Royal Stable into the gardens below.

"Look!" he said.

Far below, under a flowering cherry tree, a beautiful young pony sat among the pink blossoms. She sighed. She rubbed her head against the trunk of the tree. She tossed her mane in a girlish way.

"Oh," said the Queen. She understood everything now.

"She won't talk to me at all," said the King. "You know how it is. I thought after the last time…"

The Queen nodded her handsome head. The trouble with the princess pony these days was that she was constantly falling in love … and always with the most unsuitable ponies. At such times, she refused to speak, but she did a lot of head-tossing, sighing and sitting by herself in the garden.

Over the past year, two cart horses, a handsome but unreliable racehorse and a very shifty show jumper had all been sent away to the farthest parts of the kingdom. Each time, the pining princess had been heartbroken for about a day and a half, before another fine fetlock caught her eye.

The Queen hurried down to the garden to find out who was concerned this time. It was so tiresome. She was sure she couldn't remember being such a problem to her parents when *she* was a filly.

The Princess gave another big sigh as her mother approached. The Queen was gentle.

"Now Ponita," she said, "I know why you are moping here like this. Tell me all about it."

The Princess sighed again. "It's Prince Cavallo," she said. "He is *so* wonderful."

"But darling, you are so young," began her mother. Then she stopped. "Just a minute, did you say *Prince* Cavallo?" she asked. "You mean King Canter's son? But, my dear, why didn't you say so? He is such a charming young pony. You must invite him to the Royal Stable at once!"

The King and Queen were delighted. Prince Cavallo was an entirely suitable match for their daughter. The Prince was happy, too.

By the time lunch was over, the King and the Queen and the Prince between them had set the date and time of the wedding and decided on the flowers in the bridal bouquet.

But they had not consulted Princess Ponita. It is one thing to sigh hopelessly for a pony. It is quite another to find that the idea is not hopeless at all. As soon as she saw how well he was getting on with her parents, the Princess lost all interest in her Prince. That evening, she told her parents so.

The King tossed his head until his crown fell right off. He stamped his hoof a lot, too. But the Queen simply smiled.

"Ponita *was* much too young," she said. "We'll do just the same next time."

Too Many Princesses!

Sometimes it is nice to feel special. Of course, in lots of ways, everyone in the world is special, and it may not be a very good thing that some Princesses feel they are more special than other people. The reason they feel this is simply that there are not many Princesses about—except in Coronel, that is.

For the Kingdom of Coronel has more Princesses to the square mile than any other country in the world. The reasons for this are very complicated. You would need to read six books about royal family trees to understand it. Even most of the people of Coronel don't understand quite why there are so many Princesses about. All they know is that it is best to call a lady you have never met before "Your Highness" just in case. If she is a Princess, you have done the right thing. If not, no harm has been done.

Now, you might think that Princesses, who often feel lonely in their great castles and grand palaces, would be glad to find lots of other Princesses to be friends with. Well, some of them do, but one in particular was not pleased at all.

The Princess I am thinking of was called Melinda. She grew up in a castle in the kingdom next to Coronel, far up in the mountains. Melinda had no brothers or sisters. She was also, I'm afraid, not very fond of reading. That is why, until the time that she was a big girl of twelve, she believed she was the only Princess in the world.

I mentioned that Melinda did not like reading. In fact, she did not like any kind of learning very much. Her geography was dreadful. Her history was even worse. And as for her mathematics! It was just as well that she had so many servants to help her, for she would never have managed to add up the money in her money box by herself.

Although Princess Melinda was perfectly happy, her father the King was not. He knew that she might one day have to take charge of the castle and all the people who lived there, and he was very much afraid she would be too silly to do it properly.

One day, Melinda's father called her to him. "My dear," he said, "it is time you went to school. There is a great deal you need to learn, and it is time you made some friends among girls of your own age."

Princess Melinda did not feel very enthusiastic about going to school, but she *was* sometimes a little lonely, so when the day came, she set off happily for Coronel.

When Princess Melinda arrived at her school, the headmistress showed her to her room, which she was to share with another girl. Melinda had never shared a room before, but she thought to herself that it would be useful to have someone to clean her shoes and keep her clothes looking nice. She was very much surprised when the girl, whose name was Siska, did not seem to notice Melinda's trunk needed to be unpacked.

After ten minutes, Melinda could bear it no longer. "My clothes will be crushed and ruined," she complained, "if you don't see to them straight away."

Siska looked puzzled. "Why should I see to them?" she asked. "They're your clothes."

Melinda was so stunned she could hardly speak. "B-b-because ..." she stammered, "because I'm a *Princess*!"

"Well, so am I," replied Siska calmly. "So are most of the girls in the school."

If Melinda was stunned before, she was now so shocked she collapsed onto her bed in a heap! Another Princess? Lots of other Princesses? She felt as if her whole world was turning upside down. What was the point of being a Princess if everybody was one? It was truly dreadful.

Over the next few days, things went from bad to worse for Melinda. Not only were most of the other girls Princesses, but most of them were cleverer, prettier and more popular than she was. Melinda found she wasn't nearly as special as she had always thought. And it was not a very pleasant feeling.

Perhaps it was because she was not very happy that Melinda began to pay more attention at school. She started to read more, too. When the other girls chatted about how many diamonds they had in their coronets, Melinda had her nose in a book, learning about how coronets are made. When the other girls went dancing with the Princes at the school down the road, Melinda read a book about the history of ballrooms.

Gradually, she grew happier, until the day came when she no longer cared whether she was a Princess or not.

When Melinda was almost grown-up, the time came for her to leave school and return home. She was a very different girl now.

Her father was delighted to see how sensible and capable she had become. Over supper, Melinda outlined her plans for repairing the castle. As she went off to bed, she mentioned her ideas for improving the way that the royal lands were farmed. At breakfast the next day, she thought of a brilliant way to make the work of the portcullis-keeper much easier.

The King beamed at her across the table. "My dear," he said, "I am old and tired. No, don't say anything! It is true. Now I can do something that I have longed to do for a long time. I shall no longer be King. You will rule in my place, and I know that you will do it wisely and well. You are a very special girl indeed."

Melinda was just about to protest that she was not special at all, for there were many, many clever and accomplished Princesses, when a thought struck her. When she ruled the kingdom, she would no longer be a Princess. She would be a Queen —and there really are not very many of those in the world at all. Melinda smiled and kissed her father. There really is something very *special* about being special.

THE TWELVE DANCING PRINCESSES

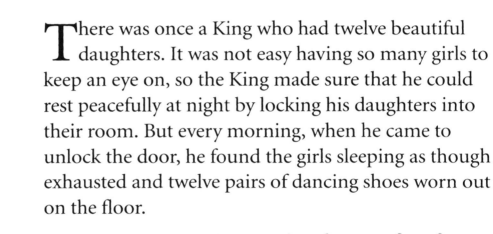

There was once a King who had twelve beautiful daughters. It was not easy having so many girls to keep an eye on, so the King made sure that he could rest peacefully at night by locking his daughters into their room. But every morning, when he came to unlock the door, he found the girls sleeping as though exhausted and twelve pairs of dancing shoes worn out on the floor.

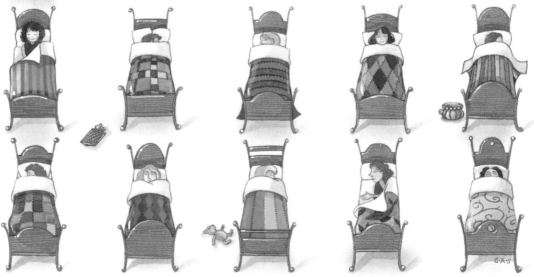

The King could not understand it. The more he thought about it, the more worried he became. At last he made a royal proclamation that whoever could solve the mystery might choose one of the girls to be his wife and become heir to the throne. But if, after three nights, the suitor was no nearer to the truth, then he must lose his life.

Several Princes came to try. They took up their posts in the hallway outside the Princesses' room and waited to see who came in. But one by one, they fell asleep and saw nothing at all. And one by one, they lost their heads.

One day, a wounded soldier passed through the kingdom. An old woman by the side of the road asked him where he was going.

Joking, the soldier replied, "Oh, I've nothing better to do, so I'm going to find out what happens to the Princesses' dancing shoes, night after night!"

The old woman looked at him for a moment and answered, "If you are serious, that is not so difficult. You must simply leave the glass of wine that is given to you in the evening, for it is drugged. Pretend to be asleep instead. Then, when the Princesses go dancing, put on this magic cloak. It will make you invisible, so that you can follow them wherever they go."

The soldier took the cloak and the advice and went on his way.

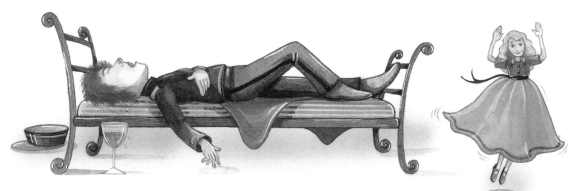

When the soldier presented himself at the palace, he was welcomed as politely as the earlier suitors. That night, he was given fine clothes to wear and shown to his bed in the hallway. The eldest Princess brought him a glass of wine, but he was careful only to pretend to drink it. Then he lay down and snored loudly to show that he was asleep.

As soon as they heard his snores, the Princesses put on their finest party clothes and jewels. They took out brand new dancing shoes and put them on their dainty feet.

Then the eldest Princess went to the head of her bed and pressed a secret panel. A passageway opened up behind it. One by one, the Princesses disappeared through the panel.

The soldier had watched all of this. Quickly, he threw on the magic cloak and went after the girls.

But in his hurry, as he followed them down the stairs, the soldier stepped on the hem of the youngest Princess's dress.

"What was that?" she cried. "Someone caught hold of me!"

"Don't be silly," the oldest Princess replied. "Come along!"

Before long, the Princesses reached the bottom of the stairs and came to an avenue of beautiful trees. Their leaves were silver and gold, gleaming in the moonlight.

"I must take some proof that I was here," thought the soldier. And he broke a twig from the nearest tree.

"What was that?" The youngest Princess heard the tiny sound.

But the eldest Princess told her to be quiet.

"Hurry along," she said. "Our Princes are waiting for us."

Next the Princesses came to an avenue of trees with diamond leaves. They sparkled and shimmered so brightly that the soldier could hardly see. Once again, he broke off a twig as evidence.

"I heard something again, I'm sure of it," whispered the youngest Princess. But once more her sister silenced her.

At last they came to a lake where twelve boats were waiting. And in each boat there was a handsome Prince. As the Princesses climbed in, the soldier joined the youngest Princess and her partner, but of course they could not see him.

"The boat feels heavy tonight," panted the Prince, as he rowed.

Across the lake stood a
wonderful castle, brightly lit.
From its open doors the
sound of music streamed
out over the water.

Laughing and talking,
the Princesses and their
Princes hurried inside, where
they were soon swept away by
the waves of music. As they danced
around the floor, the soldier danced too, but no one
could see him at all.

By three o'clock in the morning, the Princesses' shoes were quite worn out. Saying goodbye to their Princes, they hurried back to their room in the palace.

This time, the soldier went ahead of them. When the sleepy Princesses reached their beds, he was once again snoring in the hallway.

For two more nights, the soldier followed the Princesses. On the third night, instead of twigs from the sparkling trees, he brought back a golden goblet.

Next morning, he appeared before the court.

"Well," said the King, "have you found the answer to the mystery?"

"I certainly have," said the soldier, and he proceeded to tell the whole court about the secret passage, and the magic trees, and the lake, and the castle, and the dancing Princesses.

"And here," he said, producing the twigs and the goblet, "is my proof."

The King turned sternly to his daughters. "Is this true?" he asked.

Seeing that there was no way out, the girls confessed to their nightly journeys.

"Then you may choose whichever one of these troublesome girls you would like for your bride," the King told the soldier.

"I am not so young myself," the suitor laughed. "I will choose the eldest, who was so certain that there was no one following. But I am sure that all of her sisters will gladly dance at our wedding!"

So it was that a poor soldier became a great man and later King of the whole land.

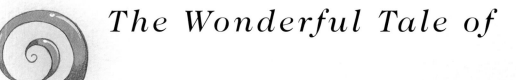

The Wonderful Tale of
THE PONY WHO FLEW

On the gentle, green slopes of the Harmony Hills, a herd of ponies grazed in the sunshine. Every now and then, they lifted their handsome heads and shook their manes in the light breeze, sniffing the soft air. All was well. No danger threatened from near or far.

Only one pony felt uneasy. It was Blue, a silvery stallion with a darker mane and tail. It wasn't because he detected a problem that the other ponies didn't. The opposite was true. Blue was restless *because* everything was fine.

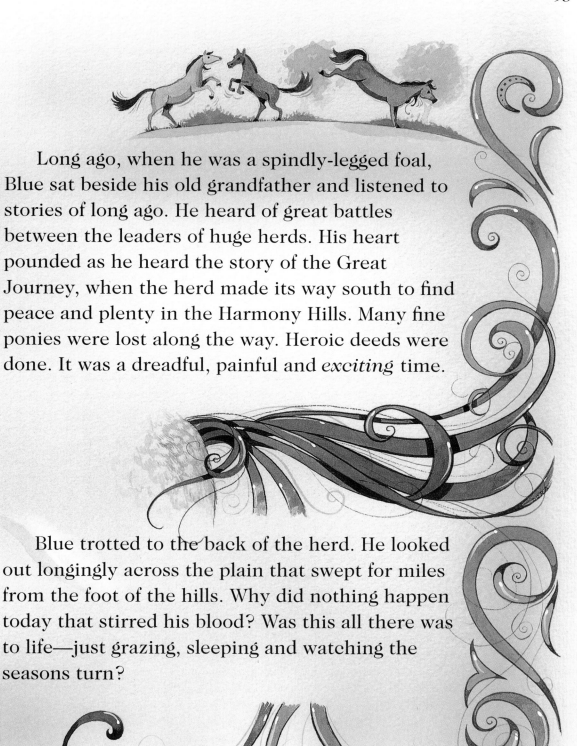

Long ago, when he was a spindly-legged foal, Blue sat beside his old grandfather and listened to stories of long ago. He heard of great battles between the leaders of huge herds. His heart pounded as he heard the story of the Great Journey, when the herd made its way south to find peace and plenty in the Harmony Hills. Many fine ponies were lost along the way. Heroic deeds were done. It was a dreadful, painful and *exciting* time.

Blue trotted to the back of the herd. He looked out longingly across the plain that swept for miles from the foot of the hills. Why did nothing happen today that stirred his blood? Was this all there was to life—just grazing, sleeping and watching the seasons turn?

Blue's mother tried to calm him. "This is the best place the herd has ever lived," she said. "There are no wolves or lions. The winters are mild and the summer sun shines gently on our backs. This is a safe place for foals to be raised and old horses to live out their lives in peace."

But Blue was still dissatisfied. One day, when the head of the herd was not looking, he trotted off into the hills and was soon lost from view in a deep valley.

The young stallion did not know what he was looking for, but he felt a shiver of fear as the steep slopes on either side hid him from the sun. It was darker and cooler here. A little stream, cold and clear, trickled along the bottom of the valley. Blue trotted beside it.

As he went, the stream widened and became a river. The ground grew rockier. He had to be careful where he placed his feet. More than once, he stumbled and almost fell.

After an hour, Blue was out of breath. At first he thought it was his own blood that roared in his ears. It wasn't until a jet of glistening spray hit his face that he looked up and saw that the thundering came from a massive waterfall, dropping like a glorious, glistening mane from the cliff edge far above. Blue had never seen anything so powerful and extraordinary.

The rushing water seemed to hypnotize the horse gazing up at it. He could not stop looking at it. And it seemed to him that in the rushing water he could see strange shapes. Suddenly, he gasped. For a moment, a rush of water seemed to him like a mighty stallion, leaping through the water, flying through the thunder.

Then Blue knew what he must do. Slowly and painfully he clambered the steep slope beside the cliff. As he climbed, his heart pounded in his chest. He had never felt so tired—or so alive.

At last the silver stallion stood on a rock at the top of the waterfall. He looked down. Surely, he thought, he could fly like the water-stallion, rushing downwards with the tumbling spray. And if he never saw the green hills of home again, at least he would have done one wonderful, extraordinary thing in his short life.

Blue tossed his head and looked up to sniff the air one more time … and all thoughts of flying vanished from his head. The view from so high was breathtaking! Blue could see across the hills and over the plain to the blue hills beyond. He could see down the river to the wide blue sea. He could see the great curving arc of the yellow shore stretching forever on either side.

There was so much more to see! There was so much more to do! The great adventure of Blue's life began right there and then. Although his four hoofs stayed firmly on the ground, his spirit flew.

It's Raining Cats and Frogs!

Magic is a wonderful thing—in the hands of a skilled magician. Unfortunately, Princess Keziah decided to have a go herself, without any training, without guidance from a wizard, without even troubling to read her book of magic from cover to cover.

"I'm a Princess," said Keziah grandly. "I don't need to bother with things like that."

Reader, she was wrong. She was terribly and dreadfully wrong. In fact, she was more wrong than when she claimed she could fly from her bedroom window (and spent several months in a plaster cast). She was more wrong than when she tried to bake a birthday cake for the Queen without reading a recipe book (and put both her parents in bed with tummy trouble for a week). Those little problems were nothing compared with the trouble she got into when she decided to try a little magic. Her governess tried to warn her, but it was no use at all.

It all started when Princess Keziah found a magic book in an old chest. When she asked her mother about it, the Queen frowned.

"I think it belonged to an old aunt of your father's," she said. "She turned herself into a caterpillar and was never seen again. Although I will say that your father's roses have never been the same since."

Keziah was excited. She hurried off at once to look at the book in her secret hideaway in the old oak tree. There must be hundreds of spells that would be useful to a young Princess!

But as Keziah reached the tree, she heard her governess calling.

"Your Highness!" called Miss Primpyprops. "Don't forget the Royal Parade this afternoon! You'll need to come inside in ten minutes to change into your best dress. Your Highness! Can you hear me?"

Princess Keziah sighed. If there was one thing she hated, it was Royal Parades. They were dreadfully boring. She would have to sit next to her parents for hour after hour as soldiers and sailors marched past in bright red and blue uniforms and shiny boots. It didn't matter how cold it was, or how hot, the Parade always went ahead. The only thing that would stop it was rain, for the soldiers were afraid the plumes on their helmets would get droopy.

Keziah looked with interest at her book. Surely a spell to bring a little rain couldn't be too difficult? She turned the pages eagerly, looking for the word "rain", and as she skimmed she suddenly saw the phrase "cats and dogs".

Now the Princess had heard her father talking about it "raining cats and dogs". This must be the spell she wanted! Unfortunately, Princess Keziah's reading was as hasty and hurried as everything else she did. She mumbled her way through the spell without pausing to think for a minute.

What happened next has gone down in the history of the kingdom. It didn't start raining cats and dogs. It started raining cats and frogs. *Real* cats and *real* frogs. Lots of them. And what with the meowing and the croaking all around, Keziah couldn't hear herself think.

Now one cuddly, fluffy cat is a lovely thing. Six cuddly, fluffy cats can be charming, too. But thousands of cuddly, fluffy cats can be too much. Much, much too much. And frogs are not everyone's cup of tea at the best of times. Hundreds of green hopping creatures underfoot can make the calmest King raise his voice and shout:

"Keziah!"

The Princess heard the shout and decided to make a quick escape. But running across the lawn would mean wading through cats and frogs. She needed to undo the spell. And fast.

Once more, Princess Keziah glanced at her book. She muttered. She mumbled. She didn't think for a second about what she was doing. And before you could say "Don't!" she had finished the whole spell.

The result was immediate, and it was better than Princess Keziah could ever have expected. Not only did the cats and frogs stop falling from the sky, they also disappeared from the grass and trees. There was no croaking and no meowing. It was wonderfully, blissfully quiet.
Until…

"Keziah!"

The King was shouting at the top of his voice.

This time Keziah hurried down the tree and across to the castle. But as soon as she stepped into the castle, she realized that there was a new problem. There were mice everywhere! Keziah was not afraid of mice, but even she didn't like to see hundreds of them at one time!

It soon became perfectly clear what had happened. When Keziah said her spell to stop the raining cats and frogs, she got rid of all cats and all frogs

everywhere, including the ones that *should* have been there. With no cats on duty in the castle, the place was overrun with mice.

The King took charge. He looked very carefully at Keziah's magic book and said a spell to put everything right.

"You see," he said, "little girls shouldn't meddle with things they don't understand. It takes a King to sort things out properly." And he took the magic book and threw it into a deep well.

And that was a pity, really. For a little frog, sitting on the edge of the well, sighed as the book fell *plop!* to the bottom.

"Meow!" he said.

The Fantastic Tale of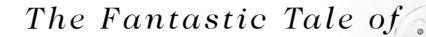

The Pony of the Sea

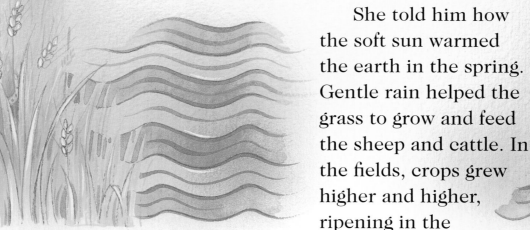

Once upon a time there was a boy who lived in a village a few miles from the coast. Half the men from the village made their living on the land. The other half were fishermen, risking their lives on the dark and dangerous sea.

Now, the boy in this story, whose name was John, was his mother's only child. She had lost her husband and her own father to the deep waters and was determined that her son should be safe. From his earliest days, she talked to him about farming.

She told him how the soft sun warmed the earth in the spring. Gentle rain helped the grass to grow and feed the sheep and cattle. In the fields, crops grew higher and higher, ripening in the

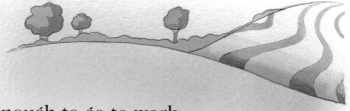

summer's heat. Then, at harvest time, the barns were filled with golden grain.

When John was old enough to go to work himself, it seemed natural to turn to the land. He loved the rhythm of the seasons and soon found he had a special talent for looking after the huge horses that pulled the carts and the threshing machines. He loved to see them toss their heads and stamp their mighty hoofs, eager to get to work. Their strength astonished him.

The horses in turn worked well for the young man. He treated them kindly, always making sure that they were comfortable and well fed before he went home for his own supper.

For five years, John worked for one of the rich farmers who owned all the land in the area. Then times became hard. The farmer called his workers together and told them he had to reduce their wages. Now the boy and his mother had only just enough to live on.

As winter drew on, a worse difficulty faced the young man. His mother became ill. The doctor shook his head and said she needed expensive medicine, but there was little money to pay for it. Night after night, John lay awake, worrying about what to do. There was only one way, he knew, to make a large sum of money quickly.

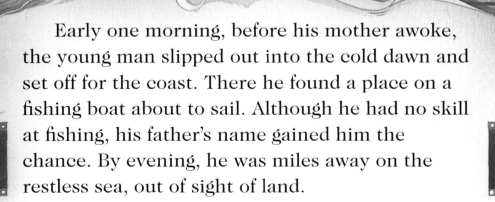

Early one morning, before his mother awoke, the young man slipped out into the cold dawn and set off for the coast. There he found a place on a fishing boat about to sail. Although he had no skill at fishing, his father's name gained him the chance. By evening, he was miles away on the restless sea, out of sight of land.

Life on board the fishing boat was unlike anything the young man had ever known. He longed to feel the solid earth under his feet again. The constant movement of the boat made him ill, and the fishermen laughed when he did not understand the words they used for parts of the boat and the work they did.

But worse was to come. Two days later, the sky grew dark and heavy. The sea heaved, making the boat creak and sway. Frightened by the faces of the fishermen, John begged them to tell him what to do. "Pray," said the skipper.

He was right. The skill of the crew and the strength of the boat were no match for the furious storm. As mountainous waves smashed down onto the boat, John's fingers were torn from the railing he clung to. He felt himself flung into the air, hurtling towards the black, boiling water.

The sea was so cold that the shock of it almost killed him. Half-conscious, he felt himself being dragged below the surface.

Then, suddenly, when he had lost all hope, John felt himself being pushed upwards. It was as though something was supporting him, something with as much strength as the sea. Through half-open eyes, he thought he saw the powerful neck of a giant horse rearing before him, its mane a stinging tangle of whipping spray. As the world grew dark around him, John clasped his arms around the sea-horse and closed his eyes.

It was many hours later that a girl, walking along the beach in the calm after the recent storm, found the young man lying on the sand. He was barely alive, but she ran for help and had him carried to her father's house.

That was the one and only time that John went to sea. It happened that the girl was the daughter of his former master.

"He's a remarkable young man," said the farmer, looking down at the sleeping youth. "Do you know that not a horse on the farm has been willing to work while he's been gone?"

His daughter smiled. She had already made up her own mind about the lad.

So John is set to become as wealthy a farmer as his father-in-law. His mother is well and happy to see her son safe home forever. But at night, when the winds howl around the farmhouse, John is quiet and grave, thinking of the poor souls out upon the stormy seas.

The Prettiest Princess

O nce upon a time, in a land far away, there lived a Princess who was very pretty. And she knew it. She grew up hearing the admiring gasps of everyone who saw her.

"How pretty she is!" "She is the loveliest little girl I've ever seen!" "Her beauty is dazzling!" Those are the kinds of things Princess Aisla heard on every side. The people who said them weren't being flattering or trying to compliment her parents. It was simply true. She was the prettiest Princess in the world.

Aisla had three sisters. Although they were all lovely girls, they looked plain beside Aisla.

Now, you might think a Princess who heard nothing but compliments all day long would be conceited and disagreeable. At the very least, you would expect her to spend hours in front of her mirror every day, brushing her beautiful hair and curling her eyelashes.

But you would be wrong. Princess Aisla was the sweetest, kindest, friendliest girl you could ever meet. And she was clever, too. Much cleverer than all her sisters.

"It isn't fair!" said Bethany one day—and not for the first time.

"I couldn't agree more," said Camilla, pulling at her perfectly nice (but not dazzling) golden hair.

"But there's nothing we can do about it," said Dahlia, frowning. "I've brushed my hair until my arm aches, and it still doesn't shine like Aisla's."

"Maybe we're going about this the wrong way," said Camilla thoughtfully. "It's not that we need to be prettier. It's that Aisla needs to be *uglier.*"

And that is why, late one night, three cloaked figures left the castle and crept down the path to the ancient Forest of Gloom.

There are no prizes for guessing how the forest got its name. Even in daylight it was a dark and scary place. At night, it was worse. The sisters trembled at every step.

Deep in the forest lived a wizard with a dreadful reputation. All little children were warned *never* to go near him. Those that did, they were told, would be turned into toads and have to live in the Forest of Gloom forever.

The Princesses came at last to the wizard's lair. Much to their surprise, he turned out to be a friendly looking old man with twinkling eyes and a half-munched cherry muffin in his hand. It wasn't what they had been expecting at all.

"There's no need to tell me why you've come, or what you're thinking," said the wizard to his visitors. "I can solve your problem in two seconds. Do you know why you were surprised by my appearance?"

"It's … well … we…" stuttered Bethany. But the wizard interrupted her.

"It's because you think someone who looks jolly and friendly must be good and kind," he said. "While someone who looks ugly and frightening must be spiteful and nasty. Well, it simply isn't true, you know. I, for example, am quite a nasty character. You're lucky to have met me *after* I've had my lunch!"

The Princesses felt uneasy. They also didn't understand *what* he was talking about.

"You mean our sister isn't good and kind?" asked Camilla, puzzled.

"On the contrary," said the wizard. "She is very good and kind, but she isn't *happy*."

"Not happy?" Such a thing had never occurred to the sisters. Surely someone who was admired so much, who was good at everything she did, who never had to worry about spots or geography homework or being unpopular, couldn't be unhappy? Could she?

The sisters hurried home through the Forest of Gloom, their thoughts whirling.

Next morning, they looked at their sister with new eyes. She was pretty. She was clever. She was loved by everyone. But it didn't mean a thing. Now they could see that she was sad inside. Suddenly, Bethany, Camilla, and Dahlia stopped hating their sister and started to want to help her.

These days, if you visit the castle on the hill beyond the Forest of Gloom, you will find four beautiful, happy sisters, and you would find it hard to tell which was the prettiest. A Princess whose eyes are glowing and heart is laughing is always lovely—and loved.

SLEEPING BEAUTY

Once there lived a King and a Queen who had no children. When, at last, a baby daughter was born to them, they were overjoyed.

"I shall give the biggest and best feast ever seen for her," said her proud father.

It seemed as though everyone in the kingdom was invited. The most important guests were the twelve fairies who make special wishes for children. In fact, there were thirteen fairies in the kingdom, but in his excitement, the King forgot to invite the last one.

At the feast, the twelve fairies gave the little girl their best gifts: beauty and riches and goodness and much more.

Just as the eleventh fairy had finished her wish, there was a crash as the great door swung open. It was the thirteenth fairy!

"So you felt you didn't need me!" she screeched. "Here's *my* present! On her fifteenth birthday, the Princess will prick her finger on a spindle and die!" And she swept from the glittering room, as a terrible silence fell.

As the guests looked at each other in horror, the twelfth fairy spoke.

"I cannot take away the curse completely," she said, "but I can make it better. The Princess *will* prick her finger, but she will not die. Instead, she will fall asleep for a hundred years."

The years passed, as years do, and the Princess grew up to be clever and kind and beautiful, just as the fairies had promised. On the morning of her fifteenth birthday, she woke up early and walked out into the castle courtyard.

It was a beautiful day. As she walked, the Princess suddenly saw the sunlight glinting on a little door that she had never noticed before. She opened it and climbed eagerly up the winding stairs inside.

At the top of the stairs was an open door, through which a very old woman could be seen as she sat, spinning.

Now the Princess had never seen anyone spinning before, for the King had banished all spindles from the kingdom when he heard the thirteenth fairy's curse.

"What are you doing, good woman?" asked the Princess, politely.

"I am spinning this fine thread," answered the woman. "Would you like to try?" And she held the spindle out to the curious girl.

"*Oh!*" cried the Princess. As she took the spindle, she pricked her finger and immediately fell asleep.

At the same moment, everyone in the castle fell asleep. The King and the Queen slept in the throne room. The servants slept in the hall. Even the cook and the kitchen dogs fell into a deep sleep.

Many, many years later ~ exactly one hundred, in
fact ~ a Prince happened to be passing the castle. It
was so overgrown with brambles that you could only
see the topmost turrets. But as he rode along beside
the high, thorny hedge, the Prince saw something
magical. Suddenly, the hedge burst into bloom!
A thousand roses spread their petals in the sunshine,
and the hedge opened to let the Prince through.

The Prince was
astonished to see all the
sleepers in the castle. At
last, he found himself in
the small room where the
Princess herself was
sleeping. He was so
dazzled by her beauty
that he bent over and
kissed her.

At that moment, the hundred years came to an end. The Princess opened her eyes, and the first thing she saw was a handsome young man, smiling down at her. Gently, he led her from the room to the courtyard below, where the whole castle was coming to life.

It was not long before the Prince and Princess were married, and the King once more gave a great feast. But this time, he was very careful indeed with his invitations!

The Mysterious Tale of
THE PONY IN THE MIST

When you live on the edge of a marsh, you can expect a winter of cold and misty weather. Old Meg was used to it. She had lived in her little cottage for over sixty years. When strange white shapes swept across the bleak landscape and clustered around her door, she was not afraid. She lit her lamps and waited until the weather cleared.

During the winter, no one ever came near Old Meg's home. Even local people could not find their way across the treacherous marsh in the fog. A stranger who tried would disappear without trace in the murky pools that lurked beside firmer ground.

Old Meg always made sure that her pantry was full and her log pile was high before the bad weather set in. This year was no exception. On the morning when she looked out of her window and could see nothing at all but the smoky, white mist, she was not at all alarmed.

The winter slowly passed. One night close to Christmas, Old Meg sat before her fire and heard a strange sound outside. She paid no attention. It might be the howling of the wind. It might be an owl swooping like a shadow across the marsh. It could not possibly be a human being.

But above the crackling of the fire, the sound came again. And again. Meg put down her knitting and listened. It sounded extraordinarily like a pony neighing.

Now, there were ponies on the marsh. They were sturdy, thick-coated little creatures who did not mind standing on soggy ground from spring until the end of autumn. But in the winter, as Old Meg knew, their owner herded them closer to his farmhouse, where he could check on them and take them extra food. There were none left on the marsh at this time of year, Meg was sure of that.

But the sound came again, and Old Meg threw her shawl about her head and opened her door. She could see nothing. Even when she fetched a lantern from inside the house, she could only see the mist swirling around her. Something was there, however. Now that she was outside, the old woman could hear not only the gently neighing but also the shifting of hoofs on the frosty ground. There really was a pony out there— and not very far away.

Old Meg had lived on the marsh too long to

take foolish risks. She feared she would be lost forever if she went out into the mist on her own, so she called to the pony, hoping it would come to her.

The pony did not move. He must be stuck or hurt, the old lady decided. Hurrying back into her cottage, she took a stout stick in one hand and a ball of her knitting yarn in the other. She tied one end of the yarn to the door knocker and set off into the mist, feeling the ground in front of her with her stick, to which she had tied a lantern.

The pony was only a few yards away. He was so much the same shade as the mist he stood in that Meg did not see him until she felt his warm breath on her face. She stretched up her hand to reassure the pony, whose big dark eyes gleamed in the lantern-light.

The pony tossed his head. He did not want to be touched. Instead, he stamped with one hoof on the ground. Old Meg looked down and gasped. Almost under the pony's hoof was a bundle of rags. It looked … no, it couldn't be … it was! There was a baby wrapped inside them.

Old Meg drove her stick into the ground and picked up the baby. She was sure it could not be alive on such a cold night, but when she buried her face in the bundle, the golden hair felt warm. Tucking the child inside her shawl, Old Meg turned to hurry back to her cottage. When she looked over her shoulder, the pony had disappeared, swiftly and silently, into the mist.

Where the tiny baby had come from, Old Meg never knew. She was a beautiful little girl. When the spring came, and the old woman could try to find out, no one could help. So Old Meg, who thought she would never have a daughter of her own, and much to the surprise of those who knew her, raised the child herself.

It was as though a light had come on in the old woman's life. She named the little girl Eleanor, and did everything for her. In the summer, Eleanor crossed the marsh each day to go to school. In the winter, she stayed at home with Old Meg, sitting beside the fire and listening to tales of long ago and far away.

It was on one of those winter evenings that the old woman told her daughter, now almost a young woman, of the mysterious pony of the mist and how she had arrived. She thought Eleanor would be astonished, but the girl simply nodded.

"I wonder," she said, "if the pony that carried me here will take me away one day. If he can bring life, perhaps he can take it."

Old Meg felt a cold fear tighten around her heart. More than anything in the world, she dreaded losing the girl who had brought light and love into her life. One day, she knew, it must happen, but she hoped with all her strength that she would not be alive to see it.

The years passed. Old Meg became very, very frail. "Don't leave me, Eleanor," she begged, when the mist swirled around the cottage once more.

"I will never leave you," promised the girl.

But one night, as they sat in the warmth of the cottage, Old Meg heard a sound that had echoed in her mind for twenty years. Desperately, she began talking, singing, laughing—anything to stop her daughter from hearing what she herself had heard. The old woman did her best, but she was weak. When she paused for breath, the neighing of a pony sounded high and clear in the icy stillness.

Eleanor rose to her feet and looked sadly at her mother. The old woman gazed into her daughter's misty eyes and suddenly smiled. In the firelight, she looked like a girl again herself.

"Oh, I was wrong to be afraid of this moment," she said. "How silly of me! Good-bye, my dear, dear girl. Remember me, wherever you go."

"I will," promised Eleanor, brushing away tears.

Then, still smiling, Old Meg pulled her shawl around her shoulders and walked out into the mist to where a strange and beautiful creature waited.

The Quest for a Kingdom

Princess Delight had only one problem. She had no kingdom. Before she was born, her father, called Prince Putoffski, had been so lazy at his Kingship Classes that his father, King Twizzle, had made a very important decision.

"You'll never succeed as a King," he said. "Your cousin, Prince Perfect, will become my heir instead. You will have to make your own living."

In the end, Prince Putoffski did make a perfectly good living as a professional ice-skater. He was happy, but, of course, he had no kingdom to leave to his only daughter, Princess Delight.

As she grew up, Princess Delight became more and more unhappy. She was not a bad skater herself, but she wasn't very interested in twirling and whirling. I'm afraid she hardly ever did any practice. No, Princess Delight didn't want to be an ice-skater. She wanted to be a real-life full-time Princess.

"The trouble is," she moaned to her father, "I can't be a Princess without a kingdom. And where am I going to find one of those?"

"That's easy!" cried her father, doing a special spin, "you need to marry a Prince. It couldn't be simpler. All you have to do is find one."

So that is why Princess Delight set off on her quest for a kingdom. She borrowed her father's second best horse and set off to look for a Prince who might just happen to have an excellent kingdom of his own.

Princess Delight rode over the mountains and along the wide river that led to the sea.

As she journeyed, the Princess met many Princes. Some were clever. Some were handsome. Some were funny. Some were silly. All of them had perfectly good kingdoms and all of them fell in love with Princess Delight. And that may have been something to do with the fact that she didn't care a bit about any of them. At least, not enough to consider marrying them.

At last, Princess Delight came to the sea. Sadly, she sat on the sand and gazed at the waves.

"I just want a kingdom," she said, "not a Prince. At least, not yet."

"Then I think I can help you," whispered a voice behind her.

Princess Delight turned. An old lady in embroidered robes was also sitting and looking out to sea.

"I am the Queen of this land," she said, "but I have no one to inherit my kingdom. It is yours, if you want it. I want to retire and take up astronomy."

Princess Delight agreed at once, but in the back of her mind there was a tiny fear. What if she didn't enjoy ruling a kingdom after all?

She needn't have worried… She *loved* it!

The Stargazing Tale of
THE PONY OF THE NIGHT

Once upon a time, there was a little pony called Daisy. She loved to kick her heels in the sunshine and gallop up and down the meadow where she lived with her mother and aunt. The older ponies smiled to see the little one so happy.

But as the shadows lengthened in the afternoon, Daisy would become quiet. There was no more rushing about or chasing butterflies. Her head drooped to the darkening green grass and she sighed unhappily.

At first, Daisy's mother, whose name was Billie, thought her daughter might be ill. A little cold perhaps? A funny feeling in her tummy? Daisy shook her head. There was nothing wrong, she said.

"It's just one of those things," said Caramel, Daisy's aunt. "I was the same when I was her age—happy one moment and sad the next. She'll be fine tomorrow."

When the same thing happened, day after day, Billie became more concerned. She took her little daughter over to a shady tree and spoke gently to her.

"You know you can tell me, Daisy, if anything is wrong," she said. "I like to see my girl enjoying herself. What is wrong?"

"Nothing," said Daisy. "Nothing at all."

"Now, Daisy," Billie insisted, "that simply isn't true. You must tell me, however embarrassing or silly it is. I won't mind."

"I'm fine," said Daisy.

Billie let the matter drop, but she had a word with her sister.

"Why don't you try talking to her?" she suggested. "Sometimes a young pony will tell an aunt things she won't tell her mother."

Caramel tried to be cheery about the whole thing, which was probably a mistake.

"Now then, Daisy," she said, "let's not have any more of this nonsense. Tell me what the trouble is and I'll fix it for you."

"You can't," whispered Daisy, and that was all she would say.

"It's a step forward," Caramel told Billie. "At least she admitted there is a problem."

"We knew that before," grunted Billie. "I'm going to have to have stern words with that girl."

Billie didn't mean to be unkind, but she was getting tired of seeing Daisy drooping about for no apparent reason. And she had given her daughter lots of chances to tell her what was going on.

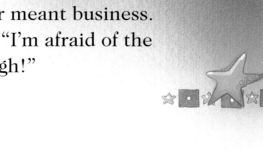

"Now, Daisy," she neighed, tossing her head firmly, "I want to know exactly what the problem is, and I want to know now. If you don't tell me at once, I will be very angry."

Daisy saw that her mother meant business.

"All right," she whinnied. "I'm afraid of the dark. There, now you can laugh!"

Billie snorted. "I'm not laughing, Daisy," she said. "Now I really am angry. No self-respecting horse or pony is afraid of the dark. It's ridiculous. Night is just the same as day—only it's dark. There's nothing to be afraid of. I don't want to hear any more about it."

But Caramel, who was grazing nearby and trying hard to look as if she wasn't eavesdropping, was reminded of something long ago.

"You know," she told her niece, "once I knew a little pony who was frightened just like you. And my mother told her something that meant she was never scared again. She told her about the pony who looks down on all of us at night and makes sure we are safe."

"Where?" asked Daisy. "How? When? Why can't I see her?"

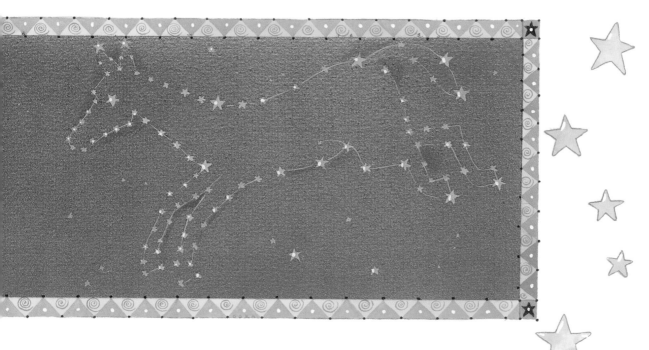

"But you can," smiled Caramel. "Wait until tonight and I'll show you."

That night, when the deep blue sky above was filled with stars, the kind aunt told Daisy to look up.

"I can only see the stars," said Daisy.

"Exactly," replied Caramel. "But if you keep looking long enough, you will see the shape of a pony, picked out in stars. Keep looking!"

Well, Daisy really did want to see the star pony, and, you know, pretty soon she was sure that she could. There it was, looking down on her!

"I don't feel frightened any more," sighed Daisy.

"Neither did the little pony I remember," said Caramel. "Did she, Billie?"

And Daisy's mother was glad that the darkness hid her blushes, as she nestled close to her little one, now smiling in her sleep.

The Lost Crown

The King looked at the Queen. The Queen looked at the Prince. The Prince looked at the Princess. And the Princess burst into tears.

"It's not my fault!" she sobbed. "I remember packing it. I wrapped it up carefully, just as you showed me, Mother, and put it right in the middle of my suitcase."

"Are you suggesting that someone has stolen it?" asked the Queen. "That would be very serious." She glared around at the servants standing nervously nearby.

"Oh no!" cried the Princess. "I've never let my suitcase out of my sight! I'm sure it's still there. Except … that it isn't!"

The King looked severely at his daughter. "You have always been a careless girl, Millicent," he said. "But losing a crown is the worst thing you have ever done. It is every Princess's duty to look after her crown. You know that."

The Princess did know that. In any case, she loved her crown. It had little pearls along the top and she knew she looked pretty in it. She certainly didn't want to lose it, but it was true that she could be careless and forgetful. She looked down at the clothes and shoes covering the floor and the furniture. Her crown simply must be there! But it wasn't.

"Well, it must be back at our Summer Palace," said the King at last, looking more kindly at Princess Millicent. "Don't cry any more, my dear. Take off your cloak and wash your face. At least we haven't lost *you*. That really would be worth crying about."

Then, as the Princess sadly took off her cloak and hood, the King, the Queen, the Prince, the maids, and the pages all began to laugh. Puzzled and upset, Millicent twirled around. As she did so, she caught sight of her reflection in a mirror—and she began to laugh as well. She was careless and she was forgetful, but she knew how to look after a crown…
It was on her head!

THE FROG PRINCE

Once upon a time, there was a King who had seven beautiful daughters. The youngest was the loveliest of them all.

On sunny days, the youngest Princess loved to play with her golden ball in a shady wood beside the castle. The sunlight sparkled through the leaves onto a cool pool nearby.

One day, when the Princess threw her golden ball high into the air, something dreadful happened. It fell … SPLASH! … into the water and sank to the bottom.

"It is lost forever!" the girl cried, but a croaky voice interrupted her.

"I could dive down and find your ball," said a little green frog by the pool, "if you would promise that I could be your friend, and share your meals, and snuggle into your little bed at night."

"Anything!" gasped the Princess hastily.

SPLISH! The frog dived into the water and soon reappeared with the golden ball.

The Princess was so delighted that she forgot all about her promise. She ran straight back to the palace, ignoring the little voice calling from the wood.

That evening, the King and his family sat down to supper. Just as they were about to start their meal, there came a croaking sound at the door. The youngest Princess tried to ignore it, but the King noticed that she looked pale.

"Who is there?" he asked.

Then the Princess explained about her promise. "But I can't let a horrible frog share my supper," she cried.

"A promise is a promise, my dear," said the King. "Let us meet your friend."

So, although the Princess shuddered every time she looked at him, the frog was allowed onto the table to share her supper.

After supper, the Princess tried to slip off to bed by herself.

"What about me?" croaked a little voice from the table. The Princess tried to pretend that she had not heard, but the King gave her a stern look.

"Remember what I said about promises," he said.

The Princess unwillingly carried the frog to her bedroom and put him down in a corner.

"I'd much rather sit on your pillow," croaked the little green creature.

Close to tears, the Princess picked up the frog and dropped him onto her pillow.

At once, the little green frog disappeared! In his place sat a handsome, smiling Prince.

"Don't be afraid," he said. "A wicked witch put a spell on me that only a kind Princess could break. I hope that we can still be friends, now that I am no longer a frog."

From that moment, the Prince and Princess became the very best of friends. In fact, a few years later, they had a wonderful wedding, and did not forget to invite some very special little green guests to join the celebrations.

The Impish Tale of

THE FAIRY PONIES

You will not be surprised to learn that fairy ponies are very small. Even the largest ones are not much bigger than a mouse. They are, of course, the perfect size for fairies, but strangely enough, you never, ever see a fairy riding a pony.

Some professors, writing on this subject, claim the reason is that, as fairies have wings, they do not need to ride. Flying is quicker and more convenient, they say.

I can tell you now that professors, for all their learning and reading, know almost nothing about fairies. The fact that these little people do not ride fairy ponies has nothing to do with flying. It has everything to do with the ponies themselves.

You see, long ago, in the days when the first fairies flitted around the earth, it didn't occur to them to try to ride on the back of an animal. I mean, you don't see rabbits trying to hitch a ride on the backs of cows, do you? Some creatures carry their little ones, it is true, but that's different. Anyway, in those days, fairies flew and ponies trotted and that was the end of the matter.

But the first human beings were not able to fly. They soon got fed up with walking around on their own two feet. It took them ages to go anywhere, and it was annoying that other animals could run faster and sometimes seemed to be laughing at the slow and lumbering humans.

One fine day, it suddenly occurred to a young human that it might be easier to let a faster animal take the strain. Of course, that wasn't the end of the story. Several very surprised ponies and a lot of bruised bottoms later, the idea was still not very practical. Human beings, however, though slow, can be determined. In the end, they found out how to ride.

The fairies, who had watched all this with interest—and, it must be confessed, a great deal of laughter—became more thoughtful. If humans could do it, why shouldn't fairies? The little people looked at fairy ponies with new eyes.

As you can imagine, the fairy ponies were less than amused when winged creatures began jumping onto their backs and shouting, "Giddy up!" It wasn't even as if fairies risked bumping their bottoms, for if they began to fall they could simply flap their wings. An Emergency Stampede—which is what fairy ponies call their meetings—was arranged at once.

"We can't have this!" neighed a famous fairy pony. "Where will it end? Before we know it, we'll be at the beck and call of those two-legged creatures all the time."

"You're right!" snuffled an elderly pony. "But what can we do to stop it? They have a huge advantage with their wings and their little fingers. They can land on your back and tangle their hands in your mane before you have a chance to spring and prance to get them off. We are simply no match for those cunning little creatures."

"I can't believe that," replied the first neigher, and his friends nodded their heads and whinnied in agreement. "We need to find their weak point, that's all."

"The only real weakness of fairies," said another pony thoughtfully, "is that they are very proud and hate to look ridiculous. But I don't see how that helps us. They are not like humans who fall to the ground with a bump all the time."

But that gave the wisest, oldest pony of all an idea. Before long, his friends were rolling on the ground and laughing.

After that, whenever a fairy jumped onto a pony's back, the clever creature didn't neigh or rear up or jump sideways. He or she simply started trotting backwards! The fairies hated it. They looked silly and they knew it. It wasn't long, much to the fairy ponies' relief, before they dropped the whole idea.

So now you know why fairies never ride. Don't try to tell those professors. They'll never believe it!

Oh, Where is my Prince?

Day after day, Princess Katerina gazed from the window of her room in the highest tower of the castle. She sighed. She did a little reading. She sighed again. She looked out at the far-off hills and mountains. She sighed once more. So it went on, day after day and month after month. And every time she sighed, Princess Katerina whispered the same words, "Oh, where is my Prince?" She felt she had been waiting for her Prince to come for years and years.

As a matter of fact, Princess Katerina was only seven! Until a few weeks before, she had loved playing in the garden, dressing her dolls and teddy bears, and playing hide and seek with her

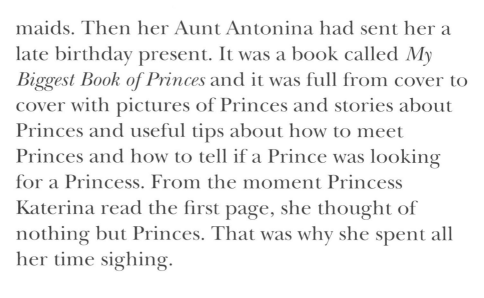

maids. Then her Aunt Antonina had sent her a late birthday present. It was a book called *My Biggest Book of Princes* and it was full from cover to cover with pictures of Princes and stories about Princes and useful tips about how to meet Princes and how to tell if a Prince was looking for a Princess. From the moment Princess Katerina read the first page, she thought of nothing but Princes. That was why she spent all her time sighing.

The King and Queen tried to talk some sense into their daughter.

"You'll have plenty of time to think about Princes later," said the King, "when you're older. Even if your Prince did come now, you couldn't marry him for years and years and years."

"Princes are all very well," said the Queen, when her husband had left the room, "but they can be a nuisance too. For one thing, they slow you down so much. It takes your father three times as long as it takes me to get ready to go out."

But Princess Katerina simply sighed again with a faraway look in her eyes.

As the weeks went by, the King and Queen discussed the problem endlessly. "Your sister Antonina got us into this mess," said the Queen at last. "She'll just have to get us out of it. We should take Katerina to see her."

The long journey to Princess Antonina's castle took six days. When they arrived, the Queen, the King, the Princess, and all their servants were exhausted. But Princess Antonina was not on the doorstep to greet them.

The High Steward bowed and explained. "Your Majesties," he said, "Her Royal Highness is in her tower room as usual. I will show you the way."

The royal party followed the High Steward through long corridors and up winding stairs. At last, out of breath and more than a little cross, they arrived at the tower room. There sat Princess Antonina, gazing from her window. Every few minutes, she sighed deeply and murmured, "Oh, where is my Prince?" When the High Steward whispered in her ear that her visitors had arrived, Princess Antonina waved a hand vaguely in their direction and sighed again.

Princess Katerina tugged her mother's hand. "She's older than *you*!" she whispered. "She must be a hundred!"

"Well, nearly forty," hissed the Queen. "She's been waiting for her Prince to come for the last thirty years."

"But where is he?"

"You know," sighed the Queen, "Princes are not always reliable. They get lost on the road a lot.

They sometimes stop off and forget where they were going. Some meet other Princesses on the way and marry them instead."

"It's not much fun waiting," confessed Katerina. "But what can a Princess do instead?"

"Anything in the world she likes." The Queen smiled. "Anything except leave muddy footprints in the throne room and go out without a proper breakfast."

I'm happy to say that Princess Katerina has done very little sighing from that day to this. Sadly, the same cannot be said for Princess Antonina…

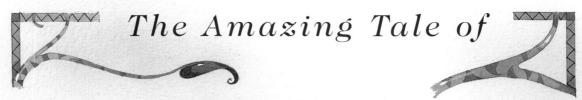

The Amazing Tale of
THE MUSICAL PONIES

Over the mountains and across the silvery sea is a land where flowers bloom and butterflies float on the scented air. There are feathery green trees, where beautiful birds settle by day and sleep by night. In sparkling streams, bright little fish flash and shine. Sunlit meadows stretch down to the deep blue sea. It is the loveliest place in the whole world. It is called Everlind.

And yet, although Everlind is the most peaceful and heavenly land you could imagine, you might not want to live there. You see, Everlind is silent. The birds do not sing. The wind does not sigh in the trees. The little streams do not chuckle and splash as they tumble over rocks. Even the sea is silent. It is very, very strange.

The tiny people who live in Everlind are perfectly happy. They are a little like elves, and even have pointy ears, but they are only for decoration. There is nothing to hear.

The Everlinders talk to each other with sign language. They have arguments and lullabies, poems and jokes, just as speaking people do. There is nothing they cannot tell each other. The Everlinders are happy in Everlind, which is just how it should be.

It was one day in late spring that everything changed in Everlind. To this day, no one knows why it happened.

A large family of tiny Everlinder people was having a picnic in a flowery meadow near a cool, deep lake. The children were playing in the grass while the grown-ups rested after lunch. Far away in the distance, a herd of the wild white ponies of Everlind were peacefully grazing. They drifted slowly nearer.

Several of the older Everlinders and a couple of the smallest had fallen asleep. The rest were playing games or chatting with their hands. In the middle of all this, in the silent sunshine, one of the white ponies drew near. He lifted up his head, opened his mouth, and sang.

Yes, he really sang. Music came out of his throat—and to our ears, it was a lovely sound, musical but deep, like the golden notes of a cello.

The confusion among the Everlinders was shocking to see. The sleepers woke up. The others stopped what they were doing and whirled around in astonishment. Then, with expressions of pain and disbelief, they clutched their ears and ran, as fast as they could, from the singing pony, gathering up their little ones but leaving all their belongings on the grass.

To the Everlinders, the noise was horrible. It seemed to travel right through their bodies, hurting them with its strangeness and power.

News of the terrible event spread quickly through Everlind. Meetings were held and votes were taken. A small party of Everlinders was chosen to go out and investigate what was happening. If only one pony was making the dreadful noise, perhaps something could be done.

The expedition was gone for two days. When it returned, its members were pale. Their hands trembled so much that they could hardly tell their friends what they had discovered.

At last the terrible truth became known. It was not only one pony that could sing. All the ponies were doing it. Sometimes, they sang together, and the sound, it seemed, was awful beyond description.

"What can we do?" asked the Everlinders.

"The world is going mad! We love our silent land. Now everything is changing."

They were terribly afraid. It was not only that strange, new sounds were invading their lives. Now, they no longer felt safe. If ponies could begin to sing, what else might happen? Would trees talk? Would butterflies chatter? Would houses laugh as they went by?

It was only a few weeks later that the second astonishing thing happened in Everlind. Visitors from another land arrived on the shore in boats. They were larger than the Everlinders but they seemed kind.

Although they, too, talked to each other with sounds, they soon began to learn to use signs to talk to the Everlinders. The tiny people, shocked by the musical ponies, were less surprised by the talking-out-loud people.

Pretty soon, the talking people became friends. The Everlinders showed them around the island— everywhere except the meadows where the singing ponies roamed.

"You won't want to go there," explained the tiny people. "It would hurt you to hear them."

But the visitors were curious. They asked to be taken to the meadows, and when their hosts refused, they set off by themselves.

The outsiders were enchanted. "These ponies are better than silver and gold!" they cried. "May we take some home with us? Their singing is glorious! They will be so admired."

"Take them all!" signed the Everlinders eagerly.

Silence returned to Everlind. The Everlinders were happy once more. And now you know why, although the singing ponies of Everlind are famous all over the world, the place that you will never ever find one is … Everlind.

The Moonstruck Tale of

THE PALACE PONIES

The King of Colomble was a proud man. Everything in his palace had to be perfect. Not surprisingly, it took him twenty years to find a wife who came up to his high standards. She turned out to be as vain and silly as her husband.

"My dear," she said at breakfast one morning, "something must be done about the palace ponies."

"Really?" The King raised an inquiring eyebrow. "But they are the finest that money can buy. And their hoofs are polished daily."

"They are white," complained the Queen. "A pretty shade of blue would be so much more stylish. Surely you can arrange that, my dear?"

The King frowned. Blue ponies would certainly look attractive. He promised to do what he could.

But the Royal Groom shook her head.

"It's impossible," she said. "The delicate skins of these perfect ponies could never be dyed. And there is no other way of making them blue."

When the King tried to argue, the Royal Groom spoke even more firmly. "Blue dye would bring them out in blisters and blotches," she said. "Surely you don't want that!"

The King shuddered at the thought. Later that day, he told the Queen what had happened. She was not sympathetic.

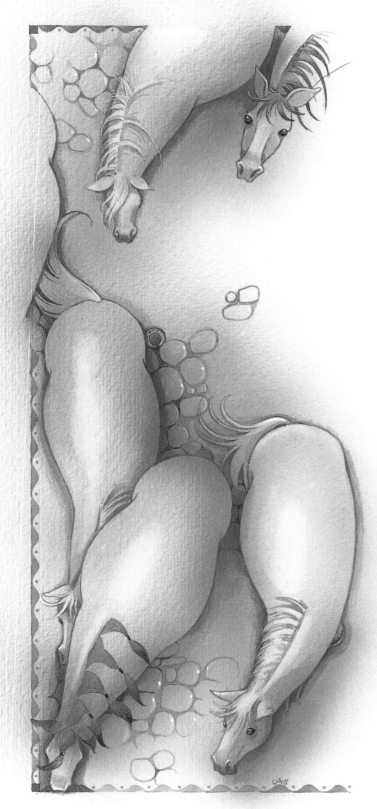

"Nonsense!" she cried. "I have the most sensitive skin in the world, and nothing has ever brought me out in blotches and blisters."

The King looked up in surprise, viewing his wife's golden ringlets with new eyes. "Do you mean…?" he began in horror.

"Certainly not!" cried the Queen, seeing that she had made a big mistake. "I will speak to the Royal Groom myself."

But that night, when she looked down from her bedroom window, the Queen had a most delightful surprise. Down in the palace courtyard, gleaming in the moonlight, were twelve ponies of the most perfect shade of pale blue. The Queen went to bed a happy woman.

The next morning, the Queen ordered her carriage. "And be sure it is pulled by the new, blue ponies," she said.

The Royal Groom came in person to speak to her mistress.

"Madam, there are no blue ponies in the stables," she said. "You are welcome to come and see for yourself."

Of course, the Queen protested. She insisted on searching every inch of the stables personally. Then she toured the extensive palace grounds. Not a single pale blue pony did she see.

The Queen had almost decided that her vision of blue ponies had been a dream when, that evening, she once more looked out of her window and saw the magical animals.

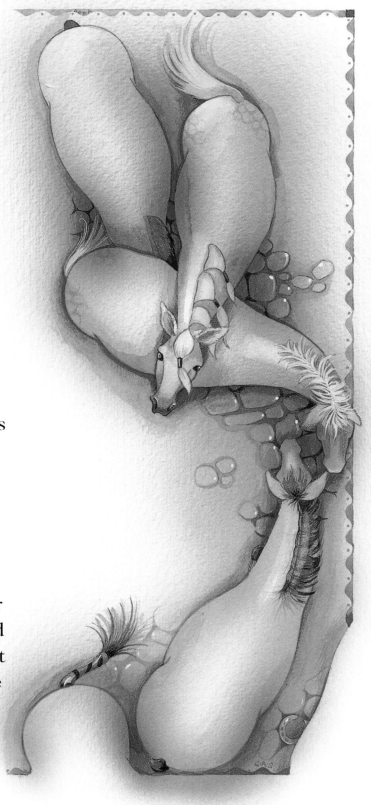

This time, the Queen wasted no time. She swept downstairs and into the courtyard, calling the Royal Groom from her bed above the stable as she went.

Out in the courtyard, the Queen beamed with satisfaction at the beautiful creatures stamping their hoofs in the moonlight.

"I suppose you will not tell me now that there are no blue ponies in the palace," she said triumphantly.

The Royal Groom opened her mouth to speak and closed it again. She knew that it was only the moonlight making the ponies appear blue, but she felt sure that the Queen would not want to be made to seem stupid—even if she was!

"You are right, Madam," she said at last. "I succeeded in finding a way of dyeing the ponies blue, but their skins are now so sensitive that they cannot go out in daylight. Only in the gentle moonlight are they safe from harm."

"I understand completely," said the Queen, reflecting that the time was fast approaching when she herself would look a great deal better by moonlight and candlelight than she would by the cruel light of day.

Ever since then, the most fashionable people in Colomble have slept by day and lived by night. Because they are also the silliest, vainest and most irritating people in Colomble, that suits the rest of the kingdom very well indeed. And the pale blue ponies of the palace keep the secret of their beauty to this day.

RUMPELSTILTSKIN

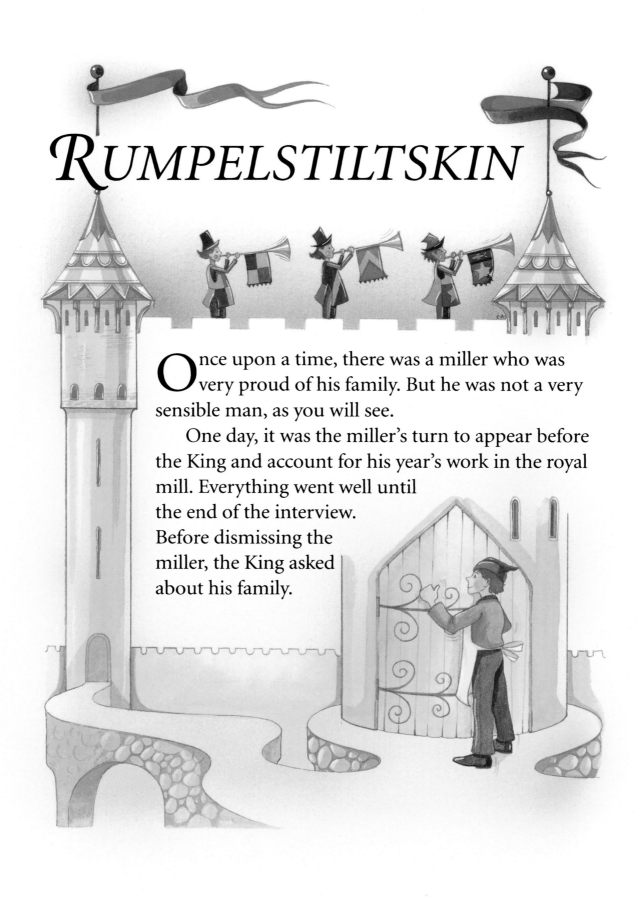

Once upon a time, there was a miller who was very proud of his family. But he was not a very sensible man, as you will see.

One day, it was the miller's turn to appear before the King and account for his year's work in the royal mill. Everything went well until the end of the interview. Before dismissing the miller, the King asked about his family.

"I hear that you have
a very pretty daughter,"
said the King.

"Not just pretty, Your
Majesty," cried the miller
with pride. "Why, she is
the cleverest girl in the
kingdom as well!"

"Really?" said the King. "Tell me, what can she do
that is so clever?"

"She … she … she … can spin straw into gold!"
blurted out the foolish miller. He had said the very
first thing that came into his head.

The King looked hard at the miller. He was very fond of money. It seemed unlikely that the girl could do as her father said, but it was worth a try.

"Bring her to the palace," said the King. "And I mean *right* away!"

So the miller went home and fetched his daughter. The King could not help noticing that she was a very pretty girl, but his mind was full of visions of gleaming gold. He took the girl to a small room, containing a spinning wheel and a huge heap of straw.

"Spin that into gold before dawn," said the King, locking the door, "or it will be the worse for you."

The girl began to cry. She had no idea what to do. Suddenly, through her tears, she saw that she was no longer alone. A strange little man stood before her.

"I may be able to help you," he said with a crafty smile, "but, of course, I will need something from you in return."

The hope that had brightened the girl's eyes for a moment faded away. "I have nothing to give you," she said.

Her visitor's sharp little eyes twinkled greedily. "Your pretty glass necklace will be payment enough," he said, and at once he set to work.

While the poor girl cried herself to sleep, the little man worked at the spinning wheel. All night long, it whirred and hummed. Before dawn, the strange little man had vanished as suddenly as he had arrived.

When he opened the door, the King was amazed and delighted to see a pile of golden thread where the straw had been.

"Tonight," he said, "I will give you a larger pile of straw. We must test your skills again."

That night, the little man once again appeared to help the bewildered girl. This time, he took the ring from her finger as payment.

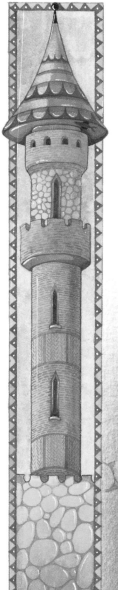

The King was a happy man. The next night, he showed the miller's daughter into an even larger room in a tower.

"If you complete your task again before morning," he said, "I will make you my Queen."

Once more, the strange little man appeared, but this time the poor girl sobbed her heart out.

"I have nothing left to give you," she explained. "Nothing at all."

The little man thought for a moment. "When you are Queen," he said, "you can give me your firstborn child instead."

What choice did the desperate girl have? Once again, the little man worked through the night.

The next morning, there was great rejoicing in the castle. The King announced his wedding to the pretty girl who had won his heart, and the miller was quite overcome with pride.

A year later, the happy young Queen rocked her first child gently in her arms. She was thinking only of the future. Suddenly, the strange little man of the year before appeared before her.

"I have come to remind you of your promise," he said.

The Queen begged him to take her jewels instead of her child, but the little man shook his head.

"I will give you one more chance," he grinned. "If you can guess my name before three nights have passed, you can keep your baby."

At once, the Queen sent out messengers to find the strangest names in the kingdom, and for the next two nights she tried every name she could think of ~ without success.

On the third night, a soldier came to her with an odd story.

"As I was riding through a wood," he said, "I saw a strange little man dancing around a fire and singing:

'The Queen can never win my game,
Rumpelstiltskin is my name!'"

That night, when the little man appeared, the
Queen said, "Is your name
Hibblehob?"

"No!" he yelled.

"Is it Grigglegreggers?"

"No, no, no!"

"Well, is it …
Rumpelstiltskin?"

The little man went red in the face. He whizzed
around and around in fury and stamped his foot so
hard that he disappeared right through the floor!

And, you know, no one has seen that strange little
man from that day to this.

The next morning, there was great rejoicing in the castle. The King announced his wedding to the pretty girl who had won his heart, and the miller was quite overcome with pride.

A year later, the happy young Queen rocked her first child gently in her arms. She was thinking only of the future. Suddenly, the strange little man of the year before appeared before her.

"I have come to remind you of your promise," he said.

The Queen begged him to take her jewels instead of her child, but the little man shook his head.

"I will give you one more chance," he grinned. "If you can guess my name before three nights have passed, you can keep your baby."

At once, the Queen sent out messengers to find the strangest names in the kingdom, and for the next two nights she tried every name she could think of ~ without success.

On the third night, a soldier came to her with an odd story.

"As I was riding through a wood," he said, "I saw a strange little man dancing around a fire and singing:

'The Queen can never win my game,
Rumpelstiltskin is my name!'"

That night, when the little man appeared, the Queen said, "Is your name Hibblehob?"

"No!" he yelled.

"Is it Grigglegreggers?"

"No, no, no!"

"Well, is it … Rumpelstiltskin?"

The little man went red in the face. He whizzed around and around in fury and stamped his foot so hard that he disappeared right through the floor!

And, you know, no one has seen that strange little man from that day to this.